The Never Girls

on
the
trail

Written by
Kiki Thorpe

Illustrated by
Jana Christy

A STEPPING STONE BOOK™
RANDOM HOUSE 🏠 NEW YORK

For Celeste and Phoebe
—K.T.
For Johnny
—J.C.

Library of Congress Cataloging-in-Publication Data
Thorpe, Kiki.
On the trail / written by Kiki Thorpe ; illustrated by Jana Christy.
pages cm. — (The Never girls ; 10)
"Disney."
"A Stepping Stone book."
Summary: "Four best friends—Kate, Mia, Lainey, and Gabby—travel to Never Land,
where they find adventure, friendship, and mystery! When the girls realize that
animal talent fairy Beck is missing, the search is on"—Provided by publisher.
ISBN 978-0-7364-3306-8 (paperback) — ISBN 978-0-7364-8168-7 (lib. bdg.) —
ISBN 978-0-7364-3307-5 (ebook)
[1. Fairies—Fiction. 2. Magic—Fiction. 3. Friendship—Fiction. 4. Mystery and
detective stories.] I. Christy, Jana, illustrator. II. Disney Enterprises (1996-) III. Title.
PZ7.T3974On 2015
[Fic]—dc23
2015009702

randomhousekids.com/disney
Printed in the United States of America
10 9 8 7 6 5 4 3 2 1

This book has been officially leveled by using the F&P Text Level Gradient™ Leveling System.

Never Land

Far away from the world we know, on the distant seas of dreams, lies an island called Never Land. It is a place full of magic, where mermaids sing, fairies play, and children never grow up. Adventures happen every day, and anything is possible.

There are two ways to reach Never Land. One is to find the island yourself. The other is for it to find you. Finding Never Land on your own takes a lot of luck and a pinch of fairy dust. Even then, you will only find the island if it wants to be found.

Every once in a while, Never Land drifts close to our world . . . so close a fairy's laugh slips through. And every once in an even longer while, Never Land opens its doors to a special few. Believing in magic and fairies from the bottom of your heart can make the extraordinary happen. If you suddenly hear tiny bells or feel a sea breeze where there is no sea, pay careful attention. Never Land may be close by. You could find yourself there in the blink of an eye.

One day, four special girls came to Never Land in just this way. This is their story.

Never Land

Pirate Cove

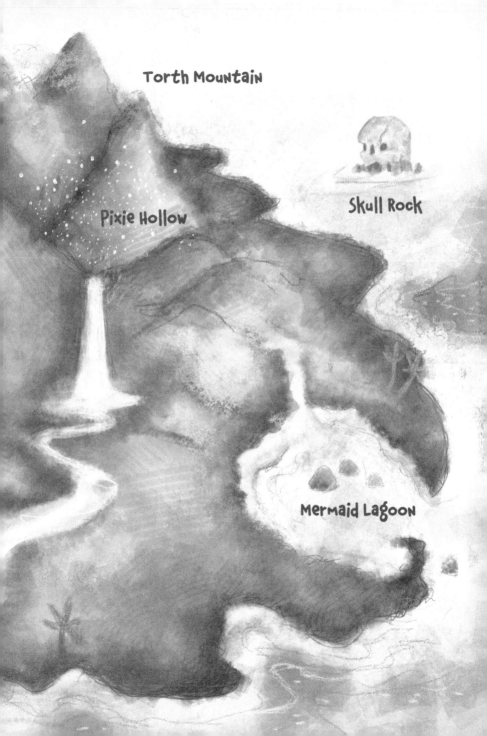

Chapter 1

Mia Vasquez stood before the oven in her kitchen. She eyed the timer above the stove. It seemed like ages since a minute had passed. She tapped the timer with her finger. Was it even working?

When she couldn't wait any longer, Mia opened the oven door and peeked at the golden brown cake baking inside.

Mia's best friend, Kate McCrady, was watching from the breakfast table. "It

won't bake any faster if you watch it, Mia,"
she said.

"Kate's right," said her other best friend,
Lainey Winters. "Watching just slows it
down."

"Is that true?" asked Mia's little sister,
Gabby, as Mia shut the oven door.

Lainey shrugged. "I don't know. But it
feels that way, doesn't it?"

That morning, the four girls had worked
together to make Mia's grandmother's
"Light as Air" angel food cake. Mia had
first learned to bake from a baking-
talent fairy named Dulcie. She loved trying out new recipes.

Beep! Beep!

Mia jumped when the timer went off.
She pulled on an oven mitt and carefully
took out the cake. As she set it on the

counter, she admired how the edges of the cake had separated nicely from the pan. To be sure it was done, Mia grabbed a toothpick and poked it into the middle of the cake. It came out spotless. *Perfect!*

The girls hovered around the cake.

Lainey leaned over and breathed in. "Mmm . . ." The steam rising from the cake fogged up her dark-rimmed glasses. "I can't see the cake, but it smells terrific."

"I want to try it now!" Kate added.

"Me too," said Gabby. "Can't we just have a teeny-tiny taste?"

"No way!" Mia said. "This cake is for the fairies."

That day, Mia was hosting her first-ever tea party in Pixie Hollow. The fairies had always been kind to them, and she wanted to do something nice in return. In her opinion, there was nothing nicer than a tea party with yummy cake.

They waited for the cake to cool. Then Mia frosted it carefully with fluffy white icing. When she was done, the cake looked even more delicious. But . . .

Mia frowned. Something was missing. *Dulcie says every recipe needs a pinch of magic,* she thought. *But what could it be for this one?*

"Why do they call it angel food cake?"

Gabby asked, interupting Mia's thoughts.

"I guess because it tastes so heavenly, angels could eat it," Mia said.

"Oh." Gabby looked disappointed. "I thought it was going to have wings."

"Like you?" Mia said, laughing. Her little sister hardly ever left the house without her costume fairy wings.

"I think it's called angel food cake because it's so light," Lainey said. "You know, 'Light as Air'?"

Mia blinked. "You guys, I think I just got an idea for how to make this cake even better."

✳

Moments later, the girls hurried up the stairs to Gabby's room. The cake had been packed into a picnic basket, along with a blanket, a thermos of tea, and Mia's mother's silver cake server.

Inside Gabby's room, Mia opened the closet door. One by one, the girls stepped through a welcoming darkness. The floor of Gabby's closet turned to earth, and the walls became curved, like the inside of a hollowed-out tree.

When they stepped out into Pixie Hollow, the sun was shining and warm against Mia's face. The girls were standing on a grassy bank. Mia followed Gabby as she hopped along the rocks to cross Havendish Stream. Lainey and Kate were close behind.

When they reached the other side, they could see the Home Tree, the great maple where the fairies lived and worked. Mia turned to her friends. "Can you start setting up for the picnic?" she asked. "I need to get the final secret ingredient."

"No problem," said Kate. "See you in the fairy circle!"

Mia hurried along the bank until she came to the mill. She could see the water wheel turning in the stream. As usual, Terence the dust-talent sparrow man was inside.

He was busy measuring out fairy dust. The sparkling dust allowed fairies to fly and do magic.

"Flying today?" Terence asked when he saw her.

"Well, not exactly," Mia said. "I was hoping I could have a pinch of dust for the tea party. You're coming, aren't you? I baked a cake!"

"I wouldn't miss it," Terence said.

As he turned, a shimmer of fairy dust floated through the air around him. He measured out a little dust for Mia, and placed it in a tiny pouch made from a leaf.

"Thanks, Terence. I'll see you soon!" Mia waved and left the dust mill. As she made her way back toward the fairy circle, something caught her eye. A rabbit was sitting by the edge of a bramble bush thicket. One of the rabbit's paws was raised as though he was hurt.

Mia stopped. She didn't want to go closer for fear of scaring him off. "Are you all right, little bunny?" she asked.

The rabbit just looked at her, wiggling its nose. Mia wished Lainey was with her.

Lainey understood animals much better than she did.

Maybe I should get a fairy to help, Mia thought. "Stay here," she told the rabbit.

Mia turned and walked briskly toward the Home Tree. Before long, a fairy with two short ginger-colored braids crossed her path. It was Beck, an animal-talent fairy.

"Beck! Beck!" Mia called, flagging her down. "Are you busy?"

"Just on my way to the fox burrow," Beck said. "Mother Fox just had her kits."

Mia told her about the wounded rabbit. "Show me where," Beck said.

Mia led the way back to the bramble bush. The rabbit was still sitting beneath it. "Oh, it's you, Dandelion!" Beck said, recognizing him.

She flittered closer and examined the rabbit's paw. "He has a thorn stuck in his foot," she told Mia. Beck reached into a pouch that was slung over her shoulder and pulled out a twig in the shape of a wishbone. "Luckily, I have my tweezers."

Beck gripped the thorn with the tweezers, speaking softly to the rabbit the whole time. Despite being hurt, the rabbit looked calm. With a flutter of her wings, Beck gave a hard yank, and the thorn came out.

"Will he be all right?" Mia asked.

Beck checked the wound and nodded. "But he'll need to lay off the paw for a bit."

"Good," said Mia, relieved. Then she stepped back. "See you at my tea party later?" she asked.

"I'll come just after I visit the kits," Beck said, barely looking up from what she was doing. "Now hold still, little guy. . . ."

Her good deed done, Mia smiled as she continued on her way. She was eager to add a little bit of her own magic to the day.

Chapter 2

Mia and her friends knelt in the fairy circle in the shade of a hawthorn tree.

Gabby, Lainey, and Kate had laid out the picnic blanket. As they set down tiny cups and plates they'd borrowed from the fairy tearoom, Mia pulled the cake from the basket. Then she reached into her pocket for the pouch Terence had given her.

"Now for the finishing touch!" Mia took a tiny pinch of fairy dust and sprinkled the glittering grains over the cake.

Too much and Mia knew the cake would be heading for the clouds. The other girls held their breath.

There!

The cake didn't move. *Hmm.* Mia frowned. *Maybe I didn't sprinkle enough,* she thought.

Just then, the cake began to rise. It floated in the air and came to a stop right in front of Mia's nose.

Gabby clapped her hands with delight.

"That is the coolest cake I've ever seen," Kate said.

"It really is 'Light as Air'!" Lainey said.

Mia laughed. "Imagine what Abuela would say if she could see this," she said.

"Just one question," said Kate. "How are you going to cut it?"

"Oh." Mia's face fell. "I guess I didn't think of that."

At that moment, the first guests arrived. The baking fairy Dulcie's glow brightened at the sight of the huge, white cake floating in the air. "Mia, this is marvelous! How did you do it?"

"It's my grandma's special recipe," Mia told her. "With a little bonus magic." She winked at Terence, who was hovering nearby. He winked back.

"We helped, too!" Gabby said.

"That's right," Mia said. "Lainey mixed

the batter. And Kate helped with the frosting."

"And I licked the bowl!" Gabby added.

"Well, I can't wait to taste it," Dulcie said.

But there was still the problem of how to serve it. When Mia tried to cut into it, the cake bobbed away through the air. The fairy circle filled with laughter as the girls took turns chasing it around with the cake server.

Tinker Bell finally had the idea of using grappling hooks to hold it steady. Several fairies hovered around, holding the cake with long ropes, while Mia sliced it into tiny pieces. By the time she'd served all the fairies, there was still plenty of cake left over.

"The best part is, you don't even need a

plate!" Dulcie said. She took a dainty bite of the cake slice floating in front of her.

Tinker Bell fluttered past, chasing a piece of cake. "This is the best tea party I've ever been to," she told Mia. "More fun than just sitting around drinking tea."

Mia smiled. Her tea party wasn't quite as she'd imagined it. But that was the great thing about Never Land—something surprising always happened.

Mia turned to reach for her own slice of cake. But it wasn't floating beside her anymore. Then she looked down and saw . . .

"That bunny is eating your cake!" Gabby exclaimed.

A soft gray rabbit was sitting on the blanket, holding down Mia's plate of cake. He was nibbling at the frosting. Everyone

had been so busy talking that no one had
noticed the new guest.

Gabby's shout startled the rabbit. In
a panic, he began to jump around the
blanket, knocking over teacups and plates.
As Kate lunged to catch him, she bumped
into the floating leftover cake, sending it
flying. Fairies screamed and dove out of
the way to avoid getting hit.

"Watch out, Gabby!" Tinker Bell yelled.

Gabby ducked just in time. The cake splattered all over the blanket.

"Help!" Mia cried. Her tea party was ruined!

"Everybody! Just. Calm. Down," Lainey commanded.

At once, the girls and fairies froze. The rabbit did, too. He sat in the middle of the blanket, surrounded by the floating mess he'd made. His body was shaking, and his whiskers and fur were covered in frosting.

"Don't be scared," Lainey said to him in a soothing voice. "We're your friends."

Myka, a scout fairy, hovered above Lainey's shoulder. "He's hurt himself, the poor thing," she said.

Mia had noticed that the rabbit was limping, too. A palm frond was wrapped around his front paw like a bandage. It was covered in frosting.

"Wait a second," she said. "This is the same rabbit I saw with Beck this morning. He had a thorn in his paw. Beck said he needed to stay off it."

"That's odd," said Terence. "Beck wouldn't let a hurt rabbit run around."

"Where *are* all the animal-talent fairies?" Kate asked.

For the first time, Mia noticed that not a single animal fairy had come to the tea party. She remembered something Beck had told her. "A mother fox had her babies this morning," Mia said. "Maybe they're all with her."

"Or Beck might be out looking for the rabbit," said the scout fairy Myka. "I'll take a look around and see if I spot her."

"I'll go to the fox hole," Tink said. "Maybe someone there can help."

"We'll stay here and keep an eye on the bunny," Lainey volunteered.

After Myka flew away, the remaining fairies helped clean up the scattered cake and the mess on the blanket. Several fairies flew back to the Home Tree with armloads of unused dishes.

Mia sighed. Her tea party hadn't turned out at all like she'd planned. *It's all that bunny's fault,* she thought. But she couldn't really be mad at the rabbit. He was too cute—and he looked too scared.

"How do we make sure he doesn't take off before the animal fairies get here?" Kate asked.

"Maybe I can try talking to him," Lainey suggested. An animal-talent fairy named Fawn was teaching Lainey to communicate with animals. Already she could speak a bit of Mouse. And once, she'd saved her friends by talking to a bear.

"Good idea, Lainey," Gabby said.

Lainey crouched down slowly to the bunny's level. "Here goes nothing," she said.

Lainey wiggled her nose at the bunny. She thumped her hands softly against the ground. Then she hopped in a circle around the blanket.

Mia bit her lip to keep from laughing. Kate was smiling, too. "Uh, Lainey, do you actually know *how* to speak Rabbit?" Kate asked.

"No," Lainey admitted with a sigh. She stood up. "But it kind of seems like it worked, doesn't it?"

Mia had to agree that the rabbit looked more relaxed. He sniffed the air, then began to wander around the picnic blanket, led by his nose. He stood on his hind legs to get at a crumb of floating cake.

"I have an idea to help him stay put," Mia said. She chased down the rest of her slice of cake and held it out to the rabbit. "Come and get it!"

Instantly, the bunny hopped over and started to nibble.

Gabby watched him eat. "Next time we should make a *carrot cake*. I bet he'd like that even more."

"I bet you're right," Mia replied with a smile. At least her unexpected guest had good taste.

Suddenly, they heard voices coming from the woods. A moment later, a group of animal-talent fairies flew into the fairy circle.

"So, this is the fella that got away?" said Fawn. She shook her head. "Oh, Dandelion, that appetite of yours is always getting you in trouble. Come on, buddy. Let's get that bandage changed and rest your foot. Where's Beck?"

"Isn't she with you?" Mia asked the fairies. "She said she was going to see the fox kits before she came to the tea party."

"We've all been with the foxes since morning," said the animal fairy Terra. "But we haven't seen Beck."

"That's strange," said Mia.

"I doubt there's anything to worry about," Fawn said. "Dandelion can be a real escape artist when he's hungry. Beck is probably out looking for him."

The girls looked at one another.

"That's what Myka thought," said Tink.

"Come along now," Fawn said to the rabbit.

Mia watched Fawn lead the rabbit away. A moment later, Myka returned—without Beck.

"No one has seen Beck since this morning," Myka reported. "I checked her room. And the mole holes. And the robins' nests—all the usual places. She hasn't left word with any of the fairies, either."

"Maybe something is wrong," Lainey said.

"Now, let's not panic," said Myka.

But Mia was starting to worry. *Where could Beck be?*

Chapter 3

Myka paced the air as she gathered her thoughts. As a scout fairy, Myka helped protect other fairies from danger. But because of her sharp senses, she also helped look for things that needed to be found—anything from lost sewing needles to missing fairies.

"Beck could be anywhere," Myka said. "There's no reason to think something bad has happened. I'm happy to go out looking for her. I'm sure she's somewhere near

Pixie Hollow. I'll find her quicker than a blink."

"I'll come with you," said Kate.

"So will I," Lainey said.

"Me too," Gabby volunteered.

"We can all help look for Beck," Mia said.

Myka considered the four girls and frowned. She was used to doing her scouting alone, or with another scout. With their dull senses and stumbling feet, she feared the Clumsies would only slow her down. But they looked so eager to help. She didn't have the heart to tell them no.

Mia was *the last person to see Beck,* Myka thought. *Maybe the girls can help after all.*

"All right," she said. "We'll start now."

"I'll get you some fairy dust," said Terence. "You might need it."

He darted away and returned a few moments later with a large portion of dust wrapped in leaves. "I double wrapped it, just in case," he said as he handed the bundle to Mia. "Fly safely."

Myka rubbed her hands together, ready to scout. There was nothing she loved more than using her talent. Even when she was worried, focusing on a task calmed her. "Mia, tell me where you last saw Beck. We'll start from there."

"I saw her by the bramble bush near Havendish Stream," said Mia.

Mia led the way. When they arrived, Myka scanned the area. A fairy scout's senses were extremely sharp. Her vision was as keen as an eagle's and her hearing was better than a bat's. As she flew, she checked all around the rocks. She checked the grass and the thicket. She listened to the flow of the stream nearby and the sounds of jays and chickadees in the trees.

The girls followed her. "What are we looking for exactly?" asked Kate.

"Anything unusual," Myka said.

Suddenly, Myka's nose picked up a strange scent. She zeroed in on the odor. "Aha! Look at this!" she called as she landed on a bramble bush leaf. There was a spot of oil-like substance on it.

Myka sniffed the leaf and felt a rush of dizziness. The oil had a strong, bitter odor.

"What is it?" asked Lainey.

"I'm not sure," Myka admitted. "But I think I know who we can ask—Elixa." Elixa was a healing-talent fairy who was always mixing up potions.

Myka removed the leaf from the
branch, being careful not to spill the oil.
"Let's go to Elixa's workshop. Follow me!"

Myka led the way back to the Home
Tree. "Wait here," she said when they
got to the pebble courtyard. She flew
through the knothole door and made her
way to the lobby, past the tearoom and
kitchen, and up through the trunk of
the tree.

Elixa's workshop was on a third-floor branch. Myka gently pushed open the wooden door and nearly fell over with dizziness. The room was filled with scents. Flowers. Herbs. Oils. Salves. It was too much for Myka's sensitive nose. She knew she couldn't stay long or she might get a headache.

Bottles of potions lined the shelves, each labeled in Elixa's precise writing. Behind a wooden counter, Elixa was carefully pouring a green substance into a vial. She didn't look up as Myka came in.

Suddenly, Mia's large face loomed in the window, peeking in. Elixa startled. "Oh! Fly with you, Mia." Then she turned and saw Myka. "You too, Myka. How can I help you today?"

Myka showed Elixa the leaf. "We found

this on a bramble bush. Do you know what this oil is?"

Elixa examined the leaf and the oily substance. "Ah, yes! Calendula, golden-seal, and oil of oregano. It's a salve for minor wounds. Best used on woodland creatures. I just mixed some for Beck today."

"When?" Mia asked through the window.

"Earlier this morning," said Elixa, look-ing back and forth between Mia and the fairy. "Is something wrong?"

"We can't find Beck," Mia told her.

"Nothing to worry about, I'm sure," Myka added quickly. "Beck must have taken the salve back to the rabbit. Do you have any idea where she might have gone after that?"

"No." Elixa frowned. "Wait! There is something."

"Yes?" Myka asked, rubbing her head. It was feeling foggy from all the different smells. She was eager to get out of the workshop.

"I told Beck she might want to have the rabbit eat some marigolds. They're good for healing," Elixa explained. "There's a big patch of them in the meadow."

Myka smiled. Now they were getting somewhere. "Can you tell me where?"

"Oh, yes. I go there often." Elixa went to the window. Myka followed, grateful for the fresh air.

"Pardon me, Mia," Elixa said, and Mia

stood aside. Elixa pointed. "Follow that path to the big meadow, and go across. The marigolds are at the far end."

"That's great! Thanks for your help," Mia said.

"Do you need anything else?" Elixa asked.

"No, I better go—by window, if you don't mind," said Myka. "You know what this place does to my senses."

"Indeed," Elixa replied. "I could give you a potion for that."

"No need," Myka said cheerfully. "I like my senses just how they are." She flew out the window to join Mia and the other girls. She was certain they'd find Beck in no time.

Chapter 4

Back in the courtyard, Mia and Myka explained to the girls what they'd learned from Elixa.

"Great!" Kate said. "So we'll start looking for Beck in the meadow."

"I'm sure we'll find her soon. Come on!" Myka said.

As she followed the scout toward the meadow, Mia noticed how strangely Myka was flying. She didn't go in a straight line. Instead, she flittered here and there, pausing to listen, look around, or sniff the air.

"Shouldn't we hurry?" Mia asked finally.

"Fast wings make slow eyes," Myka replied.

"Huh?" Mia replied.

"That's an old scout saying. It means, 'When you rush, you miss things,'" Myka explained.

"Oh. Okay," Mia said. She tried to walk slowly and notice things, but it wasn't easy. Her feet still wanted to go fast.

When they reached the meadow, Mia took in how far the grass and flowers stretched and how wide the sky seemed. Myka looked tiny in comparison to their surroundings. "The meadow is so big. How will we ever find Beck?" she said.

"The size of a place doesn't matter if you look with more than just your eyes," said Myka. "To help find Beck, open your ears to everything you hear. Smell. Touch. Taste, if necessary. But most of all, *feel*. A scout's sixth sense is sometimes her *greatest* sense."

"I thought there were only five senses," Lainey said.

"Oh no!" Myka said. "Your sixth sense is your intuition! It's helped me through the toughest scouting. When all else fails, trust your instincts."

As they crossed the meadow, Mia tried to follow Myka's advice. She listened and heard the soft breeze stirring the grass. She counted three different kinds of birdcalls. She sniffed and smelled the fresh green scent of meadow grass. There was a fainter, sweeter smell, too. Mia guessed it was some kind of wildflower. She carefully studied the plants and flowers she passed, trying to guess which one it could be.

Wait a second.

"What's this?" Mia noticed a trail of flattened grass and dirt running across their path. "Something's been through here!" she cried.

"That's a deer trail," Lainey said, coming to stand next to her. Lainey sometimes went on deer rides with Fawn.

Myka nodded. "That's right. A deer must have crossed the meadow here."

"Do you think Beck might have gone that way, too?" Mia asked.

Myka's gaze followed the trail. "Maybe," she said. "But maybe not."

"Oh. I thought it might be a clue." Mia was disappointed.

"It might be. But fairies don't need to follow paths," Myka reminded her. "Not unless they're tracking an animal, that is. Let's finish scouting the meadow and see if we can find the marigolds Elixa mentioned. We can always follow the deer trail later."

Mia thought that made sense.

The group continued on. Before long, they came to a patch of bright orange flowers.

"Marigolds!" Myka said. "This must be the patch Elixa mentioned." She flew around, examining the flowers closely. "The rabbit hasn't been here," she said at last. "Not a single petal is nibbled."

"He ended up at our tea party," Mia reminded them. "Maybe he never made it this far."

"But that still doesn't answer the question, why would Beck have left him alone?" Kate said.

"Let's look around a little more," Myka suggested.

They walked on. After a while, Mia noticed the grass was getting wetter. With every step, water seeped into her shoes. Her sneakers started to make a squelching sound.

"Why is the ground so wet?" she asked.

"We're entering a bog," Myka said. "The soil is different here. It holds more water."

The plants were different, too, Mia noticed. The tall meadow grass had given way to a stubbly sort of moss. Here and there the ground was broken by muddy pools of water.

Mia spied a strange pink flower shaped like a vase. She squatted down to take a closer look.

"That's a pitcher plant," Myka said over her shoulder. "They eat bugs."

"Bugs!" Mia exclaimed. "How?"

Myka pointed to the center of the plant. It was half filled with water. "That's a trap. The bug flies in and can't get out."

Kate leaned over Mia's shoulder to look

at the strange plant. "They don't eat fairies, do they?" she asked.

"Not that I've ever heard," Myka
replied. "Though I suppose one could if
it was big enough. But don't worry," she
added, as if she guessed what they were
thinking. "Beck's too smart to fall into a
pitcher plant."

Kate stood up and looked around.
"Should we turn back?" she asked. "Beck
probably wouldn't have come this far,
would she?"

Just then, something caught Mia's attention. A small object was stuck in the mud
nearby. "Hey!" she said. "What's that?"

She reached down and picked up a
muddied satchel as big around as her
thumb. Mia studied the bag closely. It
looked familiar. "I think this is Beck's! She

took her tweezers out of a bag just like this one when she was helping the bunny." She held the bag out for Myka to see.

Myka opened the bag and pulled out a tiny glass bottle. She sniffed the oily green contents. "This smells just like the salve that Elixa made for Beck this morning," she said.

Mia's stomach tightened. "Why would Beck's satchel be stuck in the mud?"

"Guys, look at this," Kate called. She was standing a few feet away.

The girls and Myka went over to her. Mia saw deep marks in the mud.

"It looks like an animal was here," Lainey said. "But I can't tell what kind. Can you, Myka?"

Myka shook her head. "The tracks are too smeared. But from the look of it, there was a struggle."

The girls exchanged worried looks. "Do you think the animal could have gotten Beck?" asked Kate.

"I don't know," Myka said, frowning. "Let's not jump to conclusions. After all, Beck is a very good animal fairy. If she was in trouble, she'd know how to handle it." But for the first time that day, Mia thought Myka seemed worried.

The fairy fluttered down to examine the mud again. "It's so strange. The tracks don't lead anywhere. It's as if whatever was here just disappeared right from this spot."

Mia shivered. *Vanished into thin air,* she thought. *Just like Beck.*

In the near distance was a small pond. Maybe she would find more clues there. Mia started to walk toward it. "Do you guys think we should— Ahh!" she yelled as the ground suddenly gave way beneath her feet.

Mia started to take a step forward, but her feet were stuck. The more she tried to pull them out, the deeper she seemed to sink. She screamed again as her legs were sucked down into the mud.

Chapter 5

"Help!" Mia screamed. "Help!"

"Mia!" Myka yelled. "Stop kicking! Don't panic!"

But either Mia hadn't heard her or she was too frightened to respond. She continued to flail as she slipped deeper into the bog. In no time, the mud was up to her hips.

"We're coming!" Kate started forward to help her friend.

"*Wait!*" Myka reached out to stop her and grabbed the first thing within reach, which happened to be a strand of Kate's long red hair. She gave it a hard yank.

"Ow!" Kate stopped in her tracks. She spun around and stared at Myka. "What are you doing?"

"The ground isn't safe," Myka told her. "You won't be any help if you fall in, too."

"But she's *sinking*!" Lainey exclaimed.

"Help!" Mia cried again.

"Mia, whatever you do, make sure your hands don't go under," Myka commanded. "And stop kicking—that will only make you sink faster."

To Myka's relief, this time Mia listened and obeyed. Myka turned to the other girls. "Where's the fairy dust? The extra that Terence gave you?"

Lainey looked at Kate. Kate looked at Gabby. Gabby looked at Lainey.

"Mia put it in her pocket," Gabby remembered.

They all turned to look at Mia. Her pocket was under the mud.

Oh no, thought Myka. *No, no, no.* If the girls couldn't fly to help Mia, how would they get her out? She wasn't strong enough to pull her out by herself.

Stay calm, Myka told herself. *Think.* She looked around for a branch, or a vine— anything they could use to help pull Mia out. There was nothing.

"You're going to have to crawl to her," she told the girls. "If you spread out your weight, you'll float instead of sink."

I hope, she added to herself.

"Not all at once," Myka told the girls

as they got down on the ground. "Gabby, you'll go first because you're the lightest. Kate and Lainey, you hold on to Gabby—*tightly.*"

The mud was up to Mia's middle now. Gabby inched toward her, crawling on her belly across the soggy ground. Kate and Lainey crawled after her, holding on to her feet.

When Gabby got to her sister, she grasped her hands. "Now pull!" Myka shouted.

Kate and Lainey pulled on Gabby. Gabby pulled on Mia. And Mia pulled up with all her might. There was an awful sucking sound. Then, slowly, slowly, Mia came out of the mud. A second later, she crawled onto solid ground.

As soon as she saw that her sister was safe, Gabby started to cry. "That was really scary," she said.

Mia put an arm around her. "It's okay, Gabby," she said in a shaky voice. "I'm okay now."

But it *had* been scary. Myka blamed herself. It was her job as a scout to spot every kind of danger. How had she missed this one?

I've been too caught up in looking for clues, Myka thought. She was so busy thinking about Beck that she'd missed the danger right in front of her. *From now on I'll have to be more careful,* she told herself.

"Do you think that's what happened to Beck?" Lainey asked with a shiver. "Maybe she fell in the mud and couldn't get out?"

"No," Myka said.

"How can you be sure?" asked Mia.

"Look." Myka flew over and touched down on the thin crust of soil that covered the mud. "See? I don't sink. I'm too light. I don't know where Beck is yet. But I'm certain she didn't get stuck here."

"Well, we know Beck was here, at least," Kate said. "We found her bag."

Myka nodded. It was the bag that bothered her. Why would Beck have dropped it unless she was in trouble?

She couldn't give up now. Myka decided she would send the girls back to Pixie Hollow and continue the search alone.

But when she told them, they refused. "I'm not going anywhere," Kate said. "Not until we find Beck."

"Me either," said Mia. "She might need our help. What if *you* guys hadn't been there to help me? It could be the same with Beck."

"But you can't cross the bog on foot," Myka pointed out.

Then they remembered the fairy dust in Mia's pocket. Mia's pants were still caked in mud, so she took out the pouch without much hope. But when she opened it, the dust was dry and sparkling.

"Clever Terence and his double-wrap leaves!" Myka said. She sprinkled a pinch of dust on each of the girls, which was just enough to let them fly.

"Are you sure you're okay to fly, Mia?" Lainey asked. Mia had always been a little afraid of flying.

Mia nodded. "For once I can honestly say I'd rather fly than walk."

"Then let's go." The girls rose from the ground—Kate first, then Lainey, followed by Gabby and Mia. Mia held tight to her little sister's hand.

Myka and the girls fanned out over the bog. As Myka flew, she scanned the pond. "See anything?" she called to the girls.

"All I see is moss and mud," Kate called back.

"Same here," Lainey replied.

"Nothing," said Mia.

"Me either," said Gabby.

As she flew, Myka turned over the clues in her mind—Beck's bag, the tracks in the mud that went nowhere. She couldn't make sense of it.

At the back of her mind was a fear she couldn't ignore. It was possible that an animal *had* gotten Beck. *But I don't believe it,* Myka told herself. *I won't believe it. And I won't stop looking until I figure out the truth.*

They circled the bog three times. But Myka didn't see anything that could tell her more.

The girls and Myka landed together on a patch of dry ground. Everyone looked discouraged. "What should we do now?" Mia asked.

Myka hovered, uncertain. The sea was just to the east. To the west, through the deep forest, lay Torth Mountain. Which way had Beck gone?

As she looked around, her eyes fell on something in Gabby's hand. "Gabby! Where did you get that?"

Gabby held up the feather. It was mottled gray and white with just the faintest touch of green at the tip. "I found it on the ground over there," she said, pointing. "I thought it was pretty."

Myka clapped her hands together. "It's not just pretty," she exclaimed. "It's a clue!"

Chapter 6

"How is a feather a clue?" Mia asked. There didn't seem to be anything very special about it to her.

Myka took the feather from Gabby. It was twice as tall as she was. She had to hold it with both hands. "It's a Never bird feather," she said. "I'd bet my wings on it."

"So?" said Kate.

"The Never bird is a seabird," Myka explained. "It makes its nest offshore."

"What would a Never bird feather be

doing here, then?" Lainey asked.

Myka nodded. "Exactly. That's why I think it's important. It might tell us something about Beck. At least now we know which way to go—toward the sea."

"Wait a second," Kate said. "We found Beck's bag near those animal tracks in the mud. A bird wouldn't have made tracks like that."

"That's true." Myka thought about it. "But my sixth sense is telling me to follow this clue."

Mia wished *her* sixth sense would tell her something. But the farther they went, the more uncertain she felt.

Between the bog and the sea was a narrow patch of forest. "Should we fly over it?" Kate asked. "We'll get there much faster."

But Myka shook her head. "Better stay

close to the ground. We're more likely to find her trail that way." And off she went, zigzagging through the trees.

Mia and her friends followed as best they could. Unlike the fairy, they had to duck under low-hanging branches and pick their way carefully over fallen limbs and rocks.

Mia tried her best to think and act like a scout. She listened to their steps crunch the leaves and the sounds of twigs snapping. Once, Mia spied a fairy's glow. Her heart gave a leap of hope when she thought it might be Beck. But no, it was only Myka scouting ahead.

When they finally caught up to the fairy, she was kneeling on the ground, looking at something.

"What is it?" asked Mia, going to her.

Myka held up a strand of braided grass. One end was looped like a lasso.

"That's a herding rope!" Lainey said. "The animal-talent fairies use them to catch straggling mice."

"And it's got mud on it," said Kate. "It *must* be Beck's."

Mia suddenly felt hopeful. "If Beck lassoed something, it means *she* was in control—not the other way around. Right?"

"Mmm," said Myka, only half listening. Her eyes were darting all around. Looking, looking . . .

Suddenly, she flew over to a low bush. "It went this way. See? You can tell something's been through here." She showed them a tiny twig that had been snapped completely off.

"Was it a big animal?" asked Gabby.

As Myka opened her mouth to answer, they heard the rustle of leaves. Something was moving toward them through the trees.

Everyone froze. Myka's wings beat silently as she hovered in the air. Mia could tell the fairy was listening very carefully. Even her glow seemed dimmer than usual.

What if it's a bear? Mia thought. They'd met a bear once before in Never Land. Her muscles tensed, ready to run.

Lainey must have been thinking the same thing. "Remember, if it's a bear, don't run," she whispered.

The crashing came closer. Gabby whimpered. Mia squeezed her hand.

Suddenly, Myka's glow flared again. "It's all right," she whispered, just as a large deer stepped out from the trees.

The deer froze when it saw them. For a long moment, nothing moved. The girls and the deer stared at one another in silence.

Then the deer flicked one ear and leaped away into the forest.

"Phew!" Kate's breath rushed out in relief. "Not scary."

Gabby giggled. "Not scary at all."

"It was a doe," Myka noted. "Its fawn is probably somewhere nearby. Let's keep going. The forest ends just there."

"How do you know?" Mia asked.

"Look," Myka said as she gestured ahead. "Don't you see it?"

Mia's gaze followed where the fairy was pointing. Through a break in the trees, she could see blue sky.

As they got closer, Mia began to hear a rhythmic whooshing sound. "Do I hear waves?"

"I hear it, too!" Gabby said.

"We're coming to the sea that borders Never Land to the east," Myka said.

"Maybe we'll find Beck sunning her wings on the beach," Kate said.

But when they emerged from the trees, Mia knew Kate was wrong. This was no place for sunbathing. The forest ended right at the sea—a short but straight drop down to the water. A strong wind blustered, blowing Mia's long hair around her face.

But what held Mia's attention the most lay out in the water, just offshore. "What is *that*?"

"It's called Skull Rock," Myka said.

"No kidding," said Kate.

The giant rock rose straight up from the sea. Two holes, one on either side, looked like empty eye sockets. A dark cavern formed a gaping mouth.

"I guess we hit a dead end. *Ha-ha.*" Mia laughed nervously.

The wind was making it hard for Myka to hold steady in the air. But her gaze never wavered from Skull Rock. With a sinking feeling, Mia suddenly knew what Myka was going to say.

"I think we need to go there," Myka said.

"Out to that creepy rock? *Why?*" Mia asked.

Myka landed on Mia's shoulder. "What does your sixth sense tell you?"

"I don't know," Mia replied. "But my *common* sense says 'Stay away from skeleton-shaped caves.'"

"Wait," Gabby said. "Listen! Do you hear that?"

Hear what? Mia thought. She tried to tune out the wind and the waves. Then she heard it—a high-pitched wail, almost like a baby's cry.

Maybe it was just the wind.

Then Mia heard it again. No. The sound was *alive.*

Chapter 7

Myka listened from her perch on Mia's shoulder. She could tell the crying sound was coming from Skull Rock. Whatever was making it sounded scared.

For the first time that day, Myka felt a twinge of doubt. She knew pirates often used Skull Rock to hide their ships. After what had happened in the bog, did she dare lead the girls into more danger?

And yet . . . her instincts told her that they were close to finding out what had happened to Beck. They couldn't turn back. Not now.

She glanced at Mia. Her face was tense and pale. There was no doubt about it. Mia was afraid. "You got this far," Myka whispered in her ear. "You can make it out there."

"It's not flying that scares me," Mia replied. "It's what happens when we get there that I'm worried about."

"Whatever happens, we stick together," Kate said. "Right?" She held out her hand to Lainey.

Lainey clasped it, then reached for Gabby. "Right."

"Yeah," Gabby said, taking Lainey's hand.

Kate held out her free hand to Mia. After a moment's hesitation, Mia took it.

"Okay, I can do this," she said.

They all took off.

The wind blew hard over the sea. It was difficult to make headway. Holding hands, the girls seemed to be struggling even more than Myka.

"Spread out!" Myka suggested. "Hopefully the winds will die down soon."

The girls broke apart. Kate flew out in front. Lainey and Mia were just behind her. Gabby and Myka brought up the rear.

As they came closer to Skull Rock, Myka heard the cry again. It was still faint, but clearer.

"I can hear it!" Lainey called over the wind.

Was the sound coming from inside the skull? Or somewhere nearby? Myka couldn't tell.

Just then, she noticed something bumping against the sharp rocks that jutted
up from the water near the base of Skull
Rock. It was a large nest with a wide edge
like the brim of a hat. A single white egg
was nestled inside.

The Never bird's nest! Myka's instincts
had been right! If the Never bird was here,
maybe Beck was somewhere nearby, too.

But that's strange, Myka thought, staring down at the nest. *Where is the bird? Why isn't she sitting on her egg?*

The girls hadn't noticed that Myka had stopped. "Wait!" she called after them. But her voice was lost in the wind.

She heard the cry again. It seemed different now—shriller, more urgent. And closer.

Wait a second. Myka recognized that sound. She turned in midair. Her glow almost winked out.

A huge bird bore down on her, its sharp beak open wide. The Never bird was heading right for her!

Chapter 8

Mia heard a cry behind her. She turned and saw the enormous bird racing toward Myka. Its beak looked ready to snap the fairy up.

Without thinking, Mia pushed hard against the air. She dove in front of Myka. Mia shouted and waved her arms at the bird. "Go away! Shoo!"

The Never bird screeched. Mia could feel its wings beating around her. Through a blur of feathers, Mia glimpsed the sharp rocks below. For a terrible moment she thought she would fall.

Suddenly, she felt hands close over her own. Lainey and Kate were on either side of her. "We've got you," Kate said.

Mia looked around. Where was Myka? Was she safe?

Then she spotted the fairy a few feet away with Gabby.

The bird's shrill cries filled their ears. It was coming toward them again.

"Quick! Head for the cave!" Myka cried. She and Gabby dove toward one of the big holes in the side of the rock. The rest of the girls followed.

The bird chased after them. But its wings were too wide to fit through the

opening. It flapped outside the rock for a moment, screaming in frustration. Then it flew away.

Mia's whole body was weak with relief. "That was close!" She turned to see Myka hovering in the air behind her. "Are you okay?"

"I'm fine," Myka said, though Mia could see she was shaking. "You saved me, Mia."

"That was super brave," Kate agreed.

"I've never seen you fly that fast," Lainey said.

I was *brave, wasn't I?* Mia realized in amazement. She'd done it without even thinking. "I guess I'm finally getting the hang of flying." She turned a wobbly flip in the air just for fun. "Whoa!"

Kate grabbed her arm to steady her.

"What kind of bird was that?" Lainey asked Myka.

"A Never bird," the scout answered.

"Like the feather I found!" Gabby exclaimed.

"So that means we're on the right track," Kate said. "But why did it attack us?"

Myka frowned. "I don't know. At first I thought the bird was just protecting its nest. But it kept coming after us. It's almost as if she didn't want us to come into the cave."

It suddenly dawned on Mia that they were *inside* Skull Rock. She turned to take a look around—and gasped.

They were in an enormous cavern. The cave was so wide, an entire ship could have sailed around in it. Two shafts of sunlight came through the skull's eye sockets, illuminating a deep pool of water below.

For a moment Mia forgot to be afraid. "Wow! This is *cool*!"

Her voice echoed through the cavern. Then they heard a rustling sound above them. Mia glanced up and saw dark shapes dotting the ceiling.

"Bats," Myka whispered. "Keep your voices down. We don't want to disturb them."

Mia nodded and pressed her lips together. The last thing she wanted was a bunch of bats flying around with them.

Another cry rang through the cave, making them all jump. It was the same sound they'd heard on shore.

"It's coming from there," said Lainey, pointing to the back of the cavern. All the girls could see was darkness.

"Remember," said Myka as they flew forward. "Use all your—"

"Senses," the girls whispered in unison.

Myka smiled. "You're turning into real scouts!"

As they moved away from the cave openings, Myka's glow was the only light. "Stay close," the fairy whispered.

As if I would let her out of my sight, Mia thought. She fumbled and found Gabby's hand in the dark. Lainey clutched Mia's other hand, with Kate on Gabby's other side.

Myka's glow reflected off the red minerals and green slime of the cavern walls. The air smelled salty. Water dripped from above. Each drop echoed when it hit the water below.

Suddenly, Gabby screamed.

She flew into Mia, who screamed too and knocked into Lainey. In a second the friends were all bumping into one another in a panic.

"What is it? What's wrong?" Myka exclaimed.

"Something's in here! I felt it!" Gabby said. "It's cold and wet and slimy. Don't let it get me!"

In the dim light, Mia spied a hulking form next to Gabby. Myka saw it, too. Lightning quick, she drew an arrow from

her quiver. She took aim with her bow—
and then lowered it.

"It's okay, Gabby," she said. "Look."

Myka flared her glow. Now they could
all see the big rock covered in a tangle of
sea kelp. Gabby's arm had brushed against
the kelp.

Mia laughed in relief. "It's just a rock.
It's slippery from the seaweed."

"Oh." Gabby regarded the rock warily, as if she thought it still might come after them. "Well, then what's that? Behind you?"

They all turned. Ahead in the dark was a pinprick of light.

The light grew bigger as it came toward them. A familiar voice said, "Who's there?"

"Beck!" the girls and Myka cried in unison as the pigtailed fairy came into full view.

They rushed to meet her, all of them talking at once.

"I can't believe it!"

"We've been looking for you!"

"We thought something terrible might have happened!"

Beck's eyes were round with amazement.

"How in the name of Never Land did you find me?" she asked. "Wait! Tell me later. On my wings, do I need your help!"

Chapter 9

At once, Myka took charge. She fluttered around Beck, asking, "Are you all right? You're not hurt, are you?"

"No," said Beck, "but—"

"Don't be afraid," Kate said quickly. "We won't let anything happen to you now."

"You must be exhausted," Mia chimed in. "Can you fly as far as Pixie Hollow?"

"Yes," said Beck, "but—"

"Good." Myka seized Beck's hand. She began to pull her toward the cave entrance.

"Don't worry, Beck. We'll have you back home in no time."

"Wait!" Beck yanked her hand from Myka's grasp. "What are you doing?"

Everyone stopped. They all stared at Beck. "We're *rescuing* you, of course!" Myka said.

"*I'm* not the one who needs rescuing. *She* is." Beck pointed to the darkness at the back of the cave.

"Who's *she*?" asked Kate.

"Come on." Beck flew the way she'd come, with Myka and the girls close behind. Together, the two fairy glows lit the cave faintly. Now Myka could see a narrow shelf of rock at the back of the cavern.

A baby deer was curled up at the water's

edge. It held perfectly still, watching them. Even with her sharp eyesight, Myka would have missed it if it weren't for the white spots on its back.

"Oh! It's so cute!" Gabby reached to pet the fawn's head. It gave a loud, frightened bleat. Gabby drew back, startled.

"That's the sound we've been hearing!" Kate exclaimed.

Of course! Myka thought. *It was a fawn crying.* The sound had been so out of place in Skull Rock, she hadn't recognized it.

"She's exhausted, poor thing," Beck said. "And scared out of her mind. No wonder, after all she's been through."

"But I don't understand," Myka said. "How did she get here?"

"I'll explain everything later," Beck said. "Right now I need your help. The tide is coming in. When it does, this shelf will be gone. The fawn is too worn out to swim, and I'm not big or strong enough to carry her out."

"I'll do it," said Kate, stepping forward.

But when Kate tried to pick her up, the fawn cried pitifully. She wriggled so much that Kate couldn't keep her grip. Mia tried next, but the fawn kicked her so hard with its sharp hooves that she had to let it go. Even Beck's voice didn't seem to calm the little creature.

Myka started to worry. She could see the tide *was* coming in, just like Beck said. Had they come all this way only to be no help at all?

"You try, Lainey," Mia said. "You have a way with animals."

The water was lapping at their feet as

Lainey carefully approached the fawn. She put a hand gently on its back. The deer started, but it didn't bleat or kick.

Mia heard Lainey murmuring quietly to the little fawn. Slowly, slowly, she reached her other hand around it. The fawn held still. Moments later, it was nestled comfortably in her arms.

"Lainey, you've got the special touch," Myka said.

Lainey smiled down at the fawn's head. "Maybe I do."

"Let's hurry," said Beck. "It's time we got this baby back to her mama."

They flew back through the cavern. But at the mouth of the skull, Myka stopped them. "We'd better be careful," she warned Beck. "A Never bird attacked

us on the way in. It may still be out there."

"Oh!" said Beck. "The Never bird! So she *did* find you!"

"What do you mean?" Myka asked in surprise.

"I sent her to get help," Beck said. "I told her to go to the first fairies she saw and tell them I was in the cave. She wasn't attacking you. She was trying to bring you here!"

"Well, she sure fooled us," Mia grumbled. "I thought she was going to kill Myka."

"I suppose it didn't cross my mind that the first fairy she saw might not be able to understand her," Beck admitted.

The Never bird was in her nest as they came out of Skull Rock. Beck called to her,

and the bird called back, but she didn't
move from her egg. All the same, Myka
flew a little faster as they went by.

As they flew back to shore, the wind
was with them, so the going was much
easier. On the way, Beck told them how
she had come to be in Skull Rock.

"I was with Dandelion in the meadow
this morning," she explained, "when I saw

the fawn stuck in the bog. She was really struggling. I knew I couldn't keep chasing after Dandelion when the fawn needed help."

That explains the marks in the mud, Myka thought. Beck *had* been involved in a struggle. But she wasn't fighting with an animal—she'd been trying to help!

"I couldn't get her out on my own," Beck went on. "When I saw the Never bird passing overhead, I called to her. Never birds have such powerful wings, I thought maybe she could pull the fawn out.

"I made a lasso from my rope, and we got the fawn to safe ground. But it sent her into such a panic. Rather than waiting for her mama to return, she took off through the woods. Nothing I said could calm her down." Beck sighed. "I'm afraid the Never bird made it worse. She meant to help, but she ended up scaring the fawn right into the water."

"Why doesn't that surprise me?" Kate said.

"Thankfully, fawns can swim," Beck told them. "A current carried her out to Skull Rock, and I followed. Then she was so scared, I didn't want to leave her alone. So I sent for help. But I was starting to think no one would come."

"Wow," said Lainey. "Poor little deer."

"But how *did* you find us?" Beck asked. "You still haven't told me."

"It wasn't easy. We've been on your trail all day!" Mia said.

Talking over one another, the girls

explained how they'd followed the clues, from Elixa's workshop to finding Beck's bag in the mud to the muddy lasso and the Never bird feather.

"But we wouldn't have gotten anywhere if it weren't for Myka," Mia said. "It was her sixth sense that told us to check Skull Rock."

"Myka is the best scout," Beck agreed.

Myka's glow turned pink as she blushed. The land was just in front of them. With a sigh, Myka finally allowed herself to relax. Her job was done.

Chapter 10

They had reached the shore. *And just in time,*
Mia thought. She could see that Lainey's
arms were starting to wear out. Lainey
gently set the fawn down at the edge of
the woods. For the first time since they'd
found it, the fawn stood up on its spindly
legs.

"Ohhhh," they sighed in unison. Mia
thought she'd never seen anything so
sweet.

The fawn paused for a moment. Then it bounded away. Within seconds it had disappeared into the trees.

"Will she be all right?" Lainey asked.

"She will," said Beck.

"Shouldn't we follow her, just to make sure?" asked Kate.

"No," Myka said. "Look." She pointed.

A short distance away, a doe was watching them. "It's the doe we saw in the forest."

"She's waiting until we leave to go to her baby," Beck told the girls. "She doesn't want to lead people to her fawn."

"Then we should go," Mia said.

"Bye, little deer," Lainey whispered. "I won't forget you."

They took to the air again, this time flying toward Pixie Hollow. About halfway there, Beck suddenly gave a start. "Oh, Mia!" she exclaimed. "I almost forgot! I missed your tea party! How was it?"

"Exciting!" Gabby said.

"Though maybe not quite the way I'd hoped," Mia added.

"Well," said Beck, "I'm still sorry I missed it."

Mia smiled. A new idea was taking shape in her head. "That's okay," she said. "Because my *next* tea party is going to be even better."

✳

A few days later, the woods around Pixie Hollow buzzed with excitement. Fairies zipped this way and that, following the clues that Mia had written on tiny slips of paper.

The light fairy Iridessa flew past Mia, reading her note aloud. *"Look around a mossy tree to find a pot that's fit for tea.'* Come on, Fira! There's an old moss-covered tree this way!" she exclaimed. "Let's look over there." The two fairies darted away.

Other fairies were looking for teacups

that were hidden like tiny Easter eggs amid patches of flowers. "I found the cake thingy!" Tinker Bell declared. With Terence's help, she pulled the silver cake server from the hollow of a tree.

Mia and her friends sat on a blanket in the fairy circle, watching the action. As soon as their fairy friends had found all the cups and plates and saucers, the tea party could begin.

Dulcie flew over to Mia. "You've out-done yourself this time," she said. "This treasure hunt tea party was a wonderful idea. How did you think of it?"

"From following all those clues to find Beck," Mia said. "But this time I thought the clues should lead to something fun."

"Fun—and tasty," Dulcie said, eyeing

the cake on the blanket in front of Mia. "Is it the same recipe as last time?"

"Almost," Mia said. She had made her grandmother's "Light as Air" angel food cake again. But this time she'd left out the fairy dust. Some recipes were perfect just the way they were.

As Dulcie flew off, Mia saw Queen Clarion approaching. All the girls sat up a little straighter as the fairy queen landed next to them.

"Myka told me how hard you all worked to help find Beck," the queen said. "We're all grateful."

"That's okay," said Kate. "It was fun! I mean, except for when Mia fell into that bog."

"And when we thought there was a bear in the woods," Gabby reminded her.

"And when the Never bird attacked us," Lainey added.

"And when we had to go inside Skull Rock," Mia said. But she knew what Kate meant. She wouldn't have traded their adventures together in Never Land for anything.

The queen smiled as if she understood, too. "You've shown your true fairy spirit," she said to them.

A warm glow spread through Mia. She thought she'd never felt prouder.

"Now," said Queen Clarion, "I must be off. I have a"—she checked the note in her hand—"sugar bowl to find."

The girls watched her fly away. "I can't believe the queen of the Never fairies is looking for a sugar bowl for your tea party," Kate said to Mia.

Mia laughed. "I know. But that's how it is here, isn't it?" she said. "You never know what's going to happen in Never Land."

Read this sneak peek of
A Fairy's Gift,
a special Never Girls adventure!

Mia, Kate, Lainey, and Gabby sat on the floor of the Vasquezes' living room. They were trying to play a game of Go Fish, but no one could concentrate. Mia and Gabby's aunt and uncle and their favorite cousin, Angie, were arriving for the holidays that afternoon. Every time a car went by,

Gabby interrupted the game by running to the window.

"It couldn't be them," Mia said when Gabby had jumped up a fourth time. "Mami said they'll be late because of the weather." But she got up and joined her sister at the window anyway. Fat snowflakes drifted down, covering the street in a soft white blanket. Mia watched another car slowly approach. It rolled past their house without stopping. She sighed and sat back down.

"When was the last time you saw Angie?" Lainey asked. She was shuffling the cards for another game.

"Almost two years ago," Mia said. Angie and her parents came for a week Christmas.

Mia looked forward to it every year. She'd been crushed when they'd canceled their trip the year before because they'd all come down with the flu.

"It's going to be so much fun to see her again," Kate said. "Remember that time we built a snow fort?"

"How could I forget?" Mia said, laughing. "We couldn't figure out how to make a roof, so we used the blankets from our beds. Mami was so mad when she found them in the snow."

Kate and Lainey laughed, too. "We should have told her it was a snow-pillow fort!" Lainey said.

"How come I don't remember that?" Gabby asked.

"Mami kept you inside because you had an earache," Mia said. "Also, it was two years ago. Maybe you were too little to remember."

"Was that the time Angie saw a fairy?" Gabby said.

"Oh my gosh!" Mia exclaimed. "I forgot about that!"

"What fairy?" Kate and Lainey asked in unison.

"A few years ago, around Christmastime, Angie saw a fairy right here in this room," Mia explained. "She said it flew around and knocked an ornament off the Christmas tree. When my aunt came in, it flew out the window—that's what Angie said. But Aunt Lara thought she made it up so she wouldn't get in trouble for breaking the ornament."

"How come you never told us that before?" Kate asked.

Mia shrugged. "It happened so long ago, I guess I forgot. Anyway, I never saw the fairy. I only heard about her from Angie."

"Angie said she had a pretty smile and a yellow glow," Gabby added.

Mia looked at her in amazement. "I can't believe you remember that. You must have been only two or three."

"Angie told me that if I always believed in fairies and kept my eyes open, I would see them," Gabby said. "And she was right!"

"Do you think the fairy could have been Prilla?" Lainey asked.

"I wonder," Mia said thoughtfully. There was something she'd been wondering about, but she'd been afraid to bring it up until now. "You guys, do you think maybe we could bring Angie with us? To Pixie Hollow, I mean?"

The other girls stared at her. They'd never taken anyone else to Never Land with them. It had always been their secret.

"Angie loves fairies," Mia went on quickly, before her friends could say no. "And she'd never tell anyone. She's good at keeping secrets."

"I think it's a great idea," Kate said.

"So do I," agreed Lainey.

"Yay!" Gabby clapped her hands. "The fairies are going to love her!"

"I knew you'd think so." Mia grinned. "This is going to be the best Christmas ever!"

Outside, a car door slammed. Gabby leaped up and ran to the window again. "They're here!" she shouted.

The girls scrambled to their feet. Mia ran for the front door, but Gabby got there first. She threw it open, shouting, "Merry Christmas!"

"Ho, ho, ho!" Uncle Jack boomed, scooping Gabby into a bear hug. "Merry Christmas yourself!"

Aunt Lara came through the door behind him, smiling her big smile. And finally . . . was that Angie? Mia stared. The girl who stood in the doorway stamping the snow from her boots looked nothing like the cousin she remembered. Angie had always been small, with short, messy hair. But now she was almost as tall as Aunt Lara. Snowflakes were melting into her shiny black hair, which fell past her shoulders. She wore a trim wool coat and leather boots and . . . was that *lip gloss*?

She looks so sophisticated, Mia thought. Suddenly, she felt self-conscious standing there in her old rainbow socks with the hole in one toe.

But then Angie grinned, and her smile looked exactly the same as it always had. She threw her arms around Mia, exclaiming, "I missed you!" and Mia's self-consciousness vanished.

Angie hugged Gabby, too, admiring her costume fairy wings. "They're perfect," she said. "They look just right on you." Gabby turned pink with delight.

When Mia and Gabby's parents came into the room, there was another round of hugs.

"My gosh. Look at you, Angie. You're all grown up!" Mia's mother said.

Angie smiled and tucked a strand of long hair behind her ear. "I go by Angelica now," she replied.

Angelica! Mia thought. Even her name sounded sophisticated.

"Well, Angelica is a beautiful name. I can see why you want to use it," Mrs. Vasquez replied.

Gabby grabbed her cousin's hand and began to pull her toward the stairs. "You have to come to my room right now!" she exclaimed. "We have something to show you."

Their parents laughed. "She just got here, Gabby," her father said. "At least give her a chance to take off her coat."

Gabby danced impatiently as Angelica removed her coat. "*Now* can she come to my room?" she asked as soon as the coat was hanging in the closet.

"All right, all right," Mr. Vasquez said. "You girls go have fun."

"Come on!" Gabby yanked Angelica upstairs. Mia, Kate, and Lainey followed on their heels.

"What do you want to show me, Gabby?" Angelica asked as they entered her room. "Is it a new toy?"

"Nope," Gabby said. "You'll see." She hurried over to the closet. But as she was about to open the door, Mia stopped her.

"Wait! Angie—I mean, *Angelica* should go first," Mia said. It would be even better that way.

"Into the closet?" Angelica asked with a little laugh.

"You *have* to," Gabby told her. "It's the only way to get to the fairies."

Angelica sighed. "Oh, Gabby. I'm not really in the mood to play make-believe right now."

The other girls looked at one another.

Who said anything about make-believe? Mia thought. "Just trust us," she said.

Angelica glanced from one girl to the other. "All right." She shrugged, and stepped into the closet. The others crowded in behind her—first Gabby, then Kate, followed by Lainey. Mia went in last, pulling the door closed behind her.

In the darkness, Mia smiled to herself. Any second now she'd hear her cousin's cry of surprise as she stepped out into—

"What now?" Angelica's voice was close in the dark. "What's the big surprise?"

"Ow! Gabby, you're standing on my feet!" Kate exclaimed.

"Someone's pushing!" Gabby cried back. There was a scuffling movement. The closet seemed stuffy and crowded. Where was the breeze? Mia wondered.

"Go forward!" Mia cried.

"There's nowhere to go," Angelica said. "I'm right up against the wall."

"The wall?" Mia said, confused. What was going on? Where was Never Land? She opened the closet door and they all spilled out, back into Gabby's room.

"Phew!" Angelica said as she exited, smoothing her hair. "I don't get it. Was that the game?"

Mia didn't answer. Through the open door of the closet, she could see beyond Gabby's hanging clothes to the smooth blank wall. There was no warm breeze, no window of light. The hole to Pixie Hollow was gone.